The Friend

Sarah Stewart
Pictures by David Small

Farrar Straus Giroux
New York

Annabelle Bernadette Clementine Dodd
Was a good little girl, though decidedly odd.
Belle lived every day as if she were grown—
She thought she could do *everything* all on her own.

Now Belle had a very good friend in her home
From whose sight she was seldom allowed to roam.
In fact, on most days they worked side by close side,
Where Beatrice Smith was the kindest of guides.

Belle's mother was busy—too busy to play,
And her father was much too often away.
So, hour after hour, day after day,
Belle followed Bea, with Bea leading the way.

First day of the week, they'd wash all the clothes—
Hanging them out in the sun's fullest glow.
Belle would assemble large clothespin bouquets,
While Bea would respond in her singular way:
"Glory be, Lord knows you try, my child!
Now let those clothes just flap for a while."

Then they'd walk to the beach for a swimming spree—
Belle and Bea, hand in hand, to the sea.

Second day of the week, they'd iron the shirts,
Trousers and hankies and blouses and skirts.
So Belle would sprinkle the clothes, and more—
Herself, the table, the rug, and the floor!
Bea'd straighten up, look Belle in the eye:
"Let's give this place a chance to dry!"

Then they'd hike on the beach and make art in the sand—
Belle and Bea, by the sea, hand in hand.

Third day of the week, they'd clean all the rooms.
While Bea would dust, Belle danced with her broom.
And when Belle and her broom went faster and faster,
Bea was right there to ensure no disaster.
She would stop and smile and study Belle's moves:
"Glory be, my child! Your steps are so *smooth*!"

Then they'd prance to the beach, the treasures they'd seize—
Belle and Bea, hand in hand, by the sea.

Fourth day of the week, they'd shop at the store,
And head to the garden for onions and more.
Belle would dig worms and take them all home
Where, in spite of Bea's guard, they tended to roam!
Hands on her hips, Bea'd make a strange face:
"All of God's creatures need a safe place."

Then they'd go to the beach—their castles were grand—
Belle and Bea, by the sea, hand in hand.

Fifth day of the week, they'd bake some bread
Or roll out their favorite cookies instead.
Belle was the artist and Bea was the baker.
Their tasty results seemed to cover an acre!
Bea'd turn from the stove and exclaim with pride:
"Glory be, my child! Beauty can't be denied!"

Then they'd stroll to the beach, and sit down for tea—
Belle and Bea, hand in hand, by the sea.

Sixth day of the week, they'd tackle big chores—
Washing the windows or scrubbing the floors.
But they'd only work for half the day,
With songs and jokes along the way.
When they finished, Bea'd say, "Come sit with me,
We'll look out my windows at the beautiful sea."

Then they'd climb the back stairs to Bea's tiny rooms
Filled with birds and books and sweet-smelling blooms.

Seventh day of the week, Belle was always Bea's guest.
They went to Bea's church, where Belle sang best.
And Bea would say, on this most special day:
"Hallelujah and glory be!
I'm so lucky you're next to me."

Then they'd sit in the garden and soak up the sun,
And give their thanks that the week's work was done.

But then came a day like many other days,
Except Belle snuck outside, all alone, to play.
There was no one in sight, no one at all,
So she picked up her enormous red ball.
Belle took her ball and walked straight to the sea:
"I'm the boss of myself—I'm the BOSS OF ME!"
Belle's ball bounced away, and she ran in to save it.
She felt strong and brave, until a big wave hit!

Back at home, Bea turned—where could Belle be?
Bea ran to the sea, she ran fast to the sea—

Dashed into the water in her apron and shoes—
She knew she had absolutely no time to lose!

In just a few strokes—splashing pell-mell—
Her arms were around the terrified Belle.
And out the two came, Belle and friend Bea,
Out of the great big beautiful sea.
(The ball went on to where it wanted to be.)

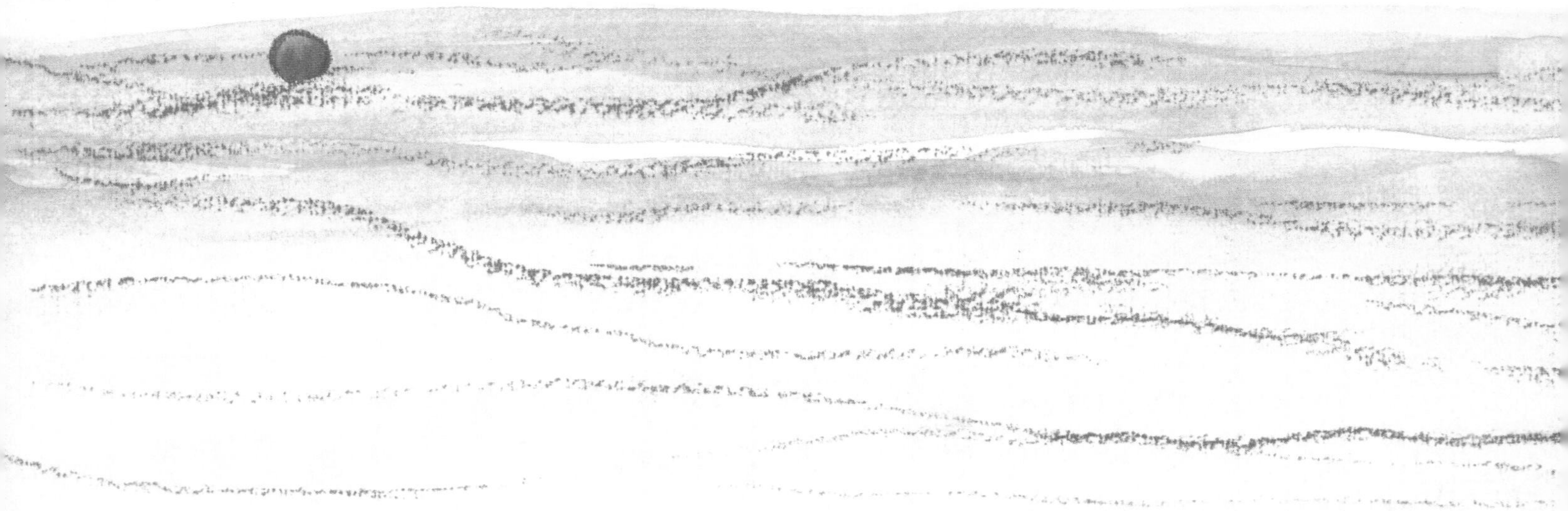

Bea carried Belle toward the kitchen's warm stove
And brought towels, hot chocolate, and cozy, clean clothes.
Belle, all dry now, and in a safe place,
Took another towel and dried Bea's face,
And wanting, most of all, to cheer her up,
Gave Bea a hug and filled up her cup.
"I'm so very, very sorry, Bea—
I should have asked you to come with me."

There was a good woman,
I called her my friend.
She's in my heart now—
She took care of me then.